W. B. Philips, Plutarco González y Torres

The Cuban Question and American Policy

W. B. Philips, Plutarco González y Torres

The Cuban Question and American Policy

ISBN/EAN: 9783337382230

Printed in Europe, USA, Canada, Australia, Japan

Cover: Foto ©Andreas Hilbeck / pixelio.de

More available books at **www.hansebooks.com**

THE CUBAN QUESTION

AND

AMERICAN POLICY,

IN THE LIGHT OF COMMON SENSE.

"*Yes, I have something more to say. There is Cuba—poor, struggling Cuba. I want you to stand by the Cubans. Cuba must be free. Her tyrannical enemy must be crushed. Cuba must not only be free, but all her sister islands. This Republic is responsible for that. I am passing away, but you must look after this. We have been together; now you must look to this.*"

       Dying Words of GENERAL RAWLINS *to Secretary Cresswell.*

NEW YORK

1869.

THE CUBAN QUESTION.

The United States Responsible for the Fate of Cuba.

The fate of Cuba rests with the United States. The Cubans have struck the blow for freedom, and for more than a year have maintained a most heroic struggle. Without effective arms or munitions of war, and without organization, preparation, or military training, they bravely proclaimed their liberty, risking their lives, property, and all they hold dear for that inestimable blessing. They were goaded to this step by intolerable tyranny and grinding exactions. They had no voice in the government over them; they were heavily taxed without their consent; they had no control over the enormous revenue exacted from them; they had not only to support a host of hungry officials in the island, who were sent out from Spain, and who had no sympathy with the colonists or interest in the colony, but they were compelled also to contribute largely to the support of their oppressors and of that very government in Europe which denied them even the shadow of political liberty. No people ever had greater cause for revolt. None ever behaved more bravely, and, considering their want of means, the difficulties they labored under, and the vast organized military power against them, none ever made greater success, within so short a period. Yet, if unaided, directly or indirectly, by the United States, the conflict must be long and doubtful, and would only end with the utter ruin of the island. Hence, as was said, the fate of Cuba rests with this country.

The Cubans may maintain the struggle to the bitter end, and, no doubt, have made up their minds to do so. The die is cast, and it would be better to suffer death in the effort to be free than to be subjugated, for Spain is cruel and unforgiving. They would have no hope in the future from the magnanimity or promises of the Spanish government. Their painful experience, throughout their whole history, of the unfulfilled promises of Spain, and the persistent refusal of that country to listen to their appeals for some show of liberality or justice, must convince them that whatever government is in power at Madrid, whether monarchical or republican, they can expect no concessions, no change for the better, no toleration. Doubtless, then, they will fight to the last, and rather than submit, carry universal desolation over the country. Their determined purpose to do this no one can doubt, who looks at the sufferings they now willingly endure, at the sacrifices they make, and at the fact that they are applying the torch to all sugar plantations and other property which might be appropriated by their enemies and used against themselves.

Nor would Spain leave Cuba without desolating it, and, as far as human power goes, making that magnificent island worthless, both to the Cubans themselves and to America, unless the United States should interpose and prevent the calamity. If the Spaniards see that Cuba can no longer be of value to them as a colony, they would do all in their power, probably, to make it valueless to others. Disgraceful as such conduct would be to any civilized nation, and to that Spain which was once so famous in history and for its chivalry, there is every reason to fear the most vindictive course toward Cuba. The statesmen of Spain—such men as Serrano and Dulce—might not desire it, but the Spaniards on the island, and the ignorant masses of the old country, who know nothing about Cuba, and are systematically deceived as to the condition of things there, would force these statesmen even to measures they might abhor. The vindictiveness, cruelty, and assumption of the Spanish volunteers in Cuba, with which the American government and people are familiar, show what may be expected in the future. A governing class or oligarchy becomes merciless in revolutionary times, when there is danger of its power and privileges being lost, and there is no people more vindictive, cruel, and reckless than the Spaniards under such circumstances.

Then, the so-called pride or haughty vanity of the Spaniards would blind them to reason and lead them to excesses even where there might be no hope of saving their fancied honor. Besides, old Spain has no sympathy with American republicanism or American progress. Notwithstanding the late revolution in

Spain, the overthrow of the Bourbon monarchy, and the profession of liberal principles, the old European prejudices and jealousy of America are strong in the Spaniards. While they profess admiration and friendship for the United States they are as jealous of this country and as ready to throw obstacles in the way of its progress as the ruling classes or governments of other countries in Europe. Nothing will be left undone, therefore, to prevent Cuban independence, the acquisition of Cuba by the United States, or the desolation of the island, so as to make it as worthless as possible to any other people than the Spaniards.

But the desolation of Cuba—the destruction of the sugar, tobacco, and other plantations, burning of towns and villages, and the ruin of all the material interests and commerce of the island—would not be the only evil of a prolonged and vindictive war, dreadful as this must prove. Want and anarchy would necessarily follow. The passions which revolution lets loose would find their vent, probably, in a war of races and factions, and we might see the horrors of San Domingo revived. The richest and most productive country in the world would be utterly ruined and left a prey to frightful disorder and carnage. The vast negro population, amounting to over half a million of souls, or near forty per cent. of the whole population of the island, are like the negroes of the Southern States, docile, peaceable, and industrious when under proper control; but they are ignorant and capable of fearful excesses, as was seen in San Domingo, when aroused by suffering or wicked leaders. Should the war continue long, and, consequently, the people be reduced to want and anarchy, there is reason to apprehend a state of things that will make the civilized world shudder. Such is the terrible prospect, unless the United States, for the sake of humanity and from a principle of high public policy, stop the war by claiming the independence or annexation of Cuba. The revolution has assumed such proportions, and all the circumstances connected with it are such that either freedom or utter ruin must be the consequence. The American republic can only decide which shall be the alternative, and upon it alone rests the responsibility.

What the United States ought to Do.

Here the question arises, then, what should the United States do in the case of Cuba ? The answer to this involves many considerations bearing upon international obligations, the material and political interests of the country, the claims of humanity, the cause of republican freedom in the world, particularly in this hemisphere, and the progress and future of the great American republic. Should the United States Government interpose to secure the independence of Cuba ? And if it should, on what grounds ? Or, taking a less decisive course, ought it to recognize the Cubans as belligerents ?. The last proposition of conceding belligerent rights would carry probably the first with it, for the American Government is not likely to take any such decided action without feeling assured that it would lead to the independence of Cuba. Nor can there be any doubt of the result should the United States recognize the Cubans as belligerents. That act alone would do much to secure the independence of Cuba. Though not bound by the mere recognition of belligerent rights to aid the Cubans the American Government would hardly permit itself to be placed in the humiliating position of seeing Cuba subjugated afterwards.

Ought the United States to recognize the Cubans as belligerents ? Nine-tenths of the American people, at least, say, yes. Probably there are none, except a few Spanish agents, and a few narrow minded men who are opposed to all progress, who would say, no. The generous and liberty-loving citizens of this great republic would proclaim at once the independence of Cuba, and act in a manner to secure it, if they would follow the noble impulses of their own hearts. There is no question as to the popular sympathy and will on this subject. It seems strange, in fact, that the government has not acted in this matter more in accordance with public sentiment, for public opinion is the basis of our republican institutions and law of our national existence. But the executive administration is naturally conservative, and properly so, as far as relates to maintaining the laws. Still, under the American form of government, the will of the people should be obeyed on great questions of national policy. There is, however, a large degree of latitude allowed to the executive in this country on all matters of an international character, and the people are disposed to be patient till they understand fully the motives or object of the government, or till their representatives in Congress can speak. With regard to recognizing the belligerent rights of the Cubans the administration has followed up to this time its conservative instincts rather than the popular will.

Is it wise to pursue that course any longer ? Has not the time arrived when the Cubans should be recognized ? Does not every consideration of national policy, interest, and humanity call for recognition ? There is no positive international law or rule of action to govern nations as to the time or circumstances when a people struggling for liberty shall be recognized as belligerents. The only principle generally acknowledged as a guide for governments in such cases, is, that those fighting for independence must have been able to sustain a war for some time with reasonable prospect of success. But each nation or government judges for itself, and that generally in accordance with its own interests or some policy it favors. Great Britain and some other European nations recognized the Confederates at the commencement, or during the first months of the late civil war in the United States. True, they did so on the plea that the magnitude of the war justified it. But a plea is never wanted whenever state policy and the supposed interests of a nation are to be promoted by such a course. The European governments looked with jealousy and disfavor upon the growing power of this republic and the consequent progress of republican ideas, and they seized the opportunity for doing what they could to dismember the country. This was their state policy. This was the State policy of monarchical Europe. Yet the Confederate States were an integral portion of a friendly and mighty nation, where all the people were free, prosperous, and happy. The South was not a distant possession or dependency like Cuba, or like the American colonies before the war of independence. There was no grinding oppression or military despotism as in Cuba on which a plea of recognition or interference could be made. The action of Great Britain and other European powers in the case of the Confederates was simply State policy based on hostility to American institutions, jealousy and national rivalry. Other examples might be cited to show, as was said, that a plea is never wanted where national interests and policy are concerned.

Not only do the powers of Europe recognize and aid revolting dependencies or sections of a country whenever it suits their purpose, but they seize and annex territories and States, depose and set up governments, for their own advantage and aggrandizement. Did not France set up an Imperial foreign government in Mexico against the will of the people on the principle of monarchical State policy? And did not the powers of Europe, Spain included, promptly recognize that government? Did not France seize large territories in Africa and appropriate Savoy? Has not England pushed her conquests over a large portion of Asia and in every part of the globe to aggrandize herself and extend her commerce? What did Prussia in Germany? What is Russia doing continually? Was not heroic Poland dismembered and parceled out among the surrounding great nations from State policy? Spain did the same as the others in former times and if she has not gone so far lately as they have, it was because she had not the power. Yet she even attempted a few years ago to reconquer San Domingo. It is absurd to talk of principle in such cases. The only principle recognized is that of national interest : the only law followed is that of the strongest : the only consideration is that of national progress, development, and grandeur. Is the great American republic to be the only power that must not study its own interests in extending its system of government, ininfluence, commerce, or territory? Shall it not take advantage of favorable circumstances, as other powers do, to fulfill its destiny and to carry out the policy of national progress? Any other great nation occupying the position this republic does with regard to Cuba would have acknowledged the the independence of that island or have annexed it long since. Yet the American government has refused up to this time to recognize the Cubans as belligerents, though that heroic people have carried on the war for independence more than a year, though they have from the smallest beginning in the sparsely settled district of Bayamo extended their conquests over the largest part of the island, and though the revolutionary government and forces are stronger and better organized to-day than ever. Upon every principle of justice, right, expediency, humanity, and national policy the United States ought to acknowledge Cuba not only as a belligerent power but as an independent republic.

The question is treated here as an American one chiefly, and from an American point of view, because whatever may be the destiny or fate of Cuba, this country has a great interest in it, and because the argument is addressed to Americans. If the island should be dessolated and ruined from the want of action on the part of the United States, the American people would suffer in their trade and commerce, the character of the nation would be damaged for permitting such a calamity, and it would lose the finest opportunity for enriching itself and developing the wealth of the Antilles. If Cuba should become an independent republic that would add another buttress, to use the simile of Mr. Seward, to the American republic and republican system, would largely increase the trade of this country, and would open a vast field for American enterprise. If the island should be annexed, that would increase the power, importance, and wealth of the United States, would give the most commanding position for naval purposes and for the domination of the whole of the West Indies, as well as the countries bordering the Gulf of Mexico and Carribean sea, and would add two or three States to the Union richer than any now possessed. It would increase greatly the variety of domestic products, give the monopoly of sugar production and other tropical productions, and would go far to make the United States independent of the rest of the world for everything that enters into the daily consumption of the people or into commerce. In fact, the rest of the world would be dependent to a great extent upon the United States for sugar and other tropical products, as it now is for cotton. Whether Cuba should be annexed or not at present, in the event of it becoming independent of Spain, there can be no doubt that in the end annexation must take place. The position of the island geographically considered and the interests of both the Cubans and the United States must lead to that. In every point of view, then, this is an American question.

The Monroe Doctrine applied to Cuba.

Forty-six years ago, when the United States were an insignificant power compared to what they are now, the government laid down as a fixed policy what is known as the Monroe Doctrine. The propositions of President Monroe in his message to Congress, December 2d, 1823, were :

First. "The American continents, by the free and independent condition which they have assumed and maintain, are henceforth not to be considered as subjects for future colonization by any European power."

Second. "The United States considers any attempt on the part of European powers to extend their system to any portion of this hemisphere as dangerous to their peace and safety."

The principle proclaimed here is, America for the Americans no European interference with the existing republican governments and progress of republican institutions on American soil, and no farther extension of the monarchical system or colonization in this hemisphere. Mr. Canning, the minister of England at the time this doctrine was proclaimed, was, in a certain sense, the author of it. He proposed it to Mr. Rush, the American minister at London, to checkmate the designs of Spain and the Holy Alliance, for subjugating and restoring the revolted Spanish colonies, which had already declared their independence. True, England had her own policy to promote by this proposition to the American government, and did not make it from any love to this republic, but that does not weaken the fact that a great English statesman saw and suggested the importance of America having a policy for itself, based upon national interests and republican institutions. But this was no new doctrine, though it assumed the official form and importance given to it by the message of President Monroe in 1823. Nearly all the statesmen of the United States up to that time, and this country was blessed with far seeing statesmen in those days, had used their efforts to prevent the extension of European influence and the European monarchical system in this hemisphere. Nor did they ever lose an opportunity to extend the area of this republic and republican institutions in

America. The early recognition of the independence of the revolted Spanish-American colonies, the acquistion of Louisiana and Florida, and other acts of the government in the earlier and purer days of its history show this. Hamilton, in 1797, tried hard to organize an invasion of the Spanish-American colonies under the protection of the United States, and in concert with General Miranda, with a view to help those colonies to their independence. And what did Mr. Monroe say, in 1812, when he was Secretary of State, to the seizing of Amelia Island and Pensacola by an American general? He advised the retaining of these places till an amicable adjustment could be made by negotiation with Spain. Doubtless this statesman had in view then the annexation of Florida. Did not the Americans in 1819, 1820 and 1821 rush, unmolested by their government, with arms and ammunition to Mexico, and very efficiently assist in overthrowing the Spanish rule there? And what was done in the liberation and annexation of Texas? Mr. Jefferson, when consulted in 1823, by President Monroe on the question of the Monroe doctrine and the action of the government with regard to the revolted Spanish American colonies, spoke of the importance of recognizing and sustaining the independence of those new States. He remarked that the independence of the United States was due to the recognition abroad of that independence. While the United States should not interfere in European affairs, he said, they should never permit Europe to intervene in America. He added, the interests of America are distinct from those of Europe, and that so long as the latter foster despotism we must secure a home for freedom upon this hemisphere. Mr. Jefferson in this same letter to President Monroe expressed the wish for the acquisition of Cuba, and said that he considered the island of great importance to the United States.

The early statesmen of the republic foresaw the mighty future of the country, and seized even opportunity to carry out its destiny. So, too, have the statesmen of other countries foreseen it. The great Napoleon, addressing the council of State in 1804, said :—" I foresee that France will be compelled to abandon all her colonies. All those in America will, within fifty years, come under the dominion of the United States ; and this conviction has led to the cession of Louisiana." A distinguished traveler and writer, M. SIMONIN, wrote, in the *Moniteur Universel*, April 11,

1868 :—" The destiny of North America is curious to contemplate. It is the country of the future to which is attracted emigration, and which is at no distant day to alter the laws of the political and commercial world." But why multiply arguments or authorities upon that which is so evident? Will the public men in the United States at the present time—will the administration and Congress, be less ready to comprehend the destiny of the country, and the opportunity that is offered in the case of Cuba?

It may be said that the Monroe doctrine does not justify the seizure of foreign possessions in this hemisphere, and the forcible dispossession of the European governments over them. No, not in time of peace, and unless the law of self-preservation demands that. But it does not mean that the government shall aid in perpetuating monarchical despotism and institutions on American soil through neutrality laws, pretended friendship to European governments, or an over sensitive regard for what is often mistakenly called national honor. It does not mean that the generous impulses of the American people shall be suppressed by their own government when they call for aid and recognition for those struggling to be free in America. It does mean, and that upon a broad principle of national policy, that every means should be used that a great nation can consistently use to secure the independence of an American people fighting to be free from European domination. It means that the United States should lose no opportunity to republicanize and Americanize this continent and the islands that belong to it, and to increase the power, influence, and commerce of this country. Never was there a case in the history of America which appealed more earnestly for the application of the Monroe doctrine than that of Cuba. The state of affairs in the island, the horrible despotism of Spain over it, the frightful cruelty of the Spaniards in the war, the prolonged and heroic struggle of the Cubans, their successes under the greatest difficulties, their ability to sustain the war, the cry of anguish from the suffering people, their touching appeals to and hope from the United States, the political and commercial interests of this country that are involved, the progress of American freedom and republican institutions—all call for the sympathy and interposition of the American people and government. The exclusion of Spain from Cuba should be the determined policy of the United States.

Let the Cubans be recognized as belligerents—yes, let their independence be acknowledged—and let the generous and liberty-loving American people go to their aid, and the war will soon be over, and Cuba saved from the fate of San Domingo.

No doubt the independence of Cuba would lead, as was said before, to its annexation to the United States. Whether it should or not the argument in favor of American action is the same. In addition to the views of American statesmen and eminent men, which have been given, with regard to the importance or value of Cuba to the United States, those of Mr. Edward Everett, as expressed when he was Secretary of State, in his famous reply to the French and British governments on the tripartite treaty proposition, may be cited. He remarks:—" Territorially and commercially it would, in our hands, be an extremely valuable possession. In certain contingencies it might be almost essential to our safety." Again:—" There is at the present time an evident tendency in the maritime commerce of the world, to avail itself of the shortest passages from one ocean to another, offered by the different routes existing or in contemplation across the isthmus of Central America. The island of Cuba, of considerable importance in itself, is so placed geographically, that the nation which may possess it, if the naval forces of that nation should be considerable, might either protect or obstruct the commercial routes from one ocean to the other." In another place he says:—" The United States, on the other hand, would, by the proposed convention (tripartite treaty) disable themselves from making an acquisition which might take place without any disturbance of existing foreign relations, and in the natural order of things. The island of Cuba lies at our doors. It commands the approach to the Gulf of Mexico, which washes the shores of five States. It bars the entrance of that great river which drains half the North American continent, and, with its tributaries, forms the largest system of internal water communication in the world. It keeps watch at the door-way of our intercourse with California by the Isthmus route. If an island like Cuba, belonging to the Spanish crown, guarded the entrance to the Thames or the Seine, and the United States should propose a convention like this to France and England, those powers would assuredly feel that the disability assumed by ourselves was far less serious than that which we asked them to assume." Mr. Everett might have added, had he not been writing a diplomatic note, that if Cuba lay across the mouth of the Thames or the Seine, or guarded any other great outlet of British or French commerce, it would have been seized by either of these powers long ago. It would not have taken long before national interests would have overruled their national honor or regard for the nation in possession of such an island.

The Trade and Resources of Cuba.

The value of Cuba to the United States as the key to the Gulf of Mexico, as dominating the West Indies, as a protection to the coast and trade of this country on the Gulf, as extending American influence over the whole region bordering the Carribean sea and the Gulf of Mexico, and in fact, as making the latter simply an American lake, has been adverted to, as well as the commercial value of that island to this country. It will be well, however, to call attention particularly to the productions, trade and prospective resources of Cuba.

According to an estimate made up from reliable data, the imports and exports of Cuba for the year just preceding the revolution, and, therefore, while the island was in its normal condition, were :—

IMPORTS............ ....$64,000,000
EXPORTS.... 80,000,000

TOTAL $144,000,000

In 1859, according to Pezuela's Geographical and Statistical Distionary, they were:—

IMPORTS...... .... $43,465,976
EXPORTS..... 57,455,185

TOTAL........$100,920,864

Taking the statistical report of Dr. Jose Maria de la Torre for the three years from 1861 to 1863, the average yearly total imports and exports were, $130,000,000.

The total imports and exports then have increased steadily at about the rate of fifty per cent. in the ten years since 1859. It must be remembered that this large and valuable trade has been developed under the most unfavorable circumstances—under the high tariff, repressive government, and grinding exactions imposed by Spain. It shows, however, the vast wealth and importance of the commerce of Cuba. Had that island been under the beneficent and liberal government of the United States, the trade would have been doubled probably, and would have amounted to three hundred millions at least instead of a hundred and fifty millions.

The importance of the commerce with Cuba may be appreciated by referring to a table of statistics by Fernandez Corredor, showing the relative proportion among the different commercial nations. It is as follows :—

United States of America	35.94	per Cent.
England	22.52	"
Spain	19.48	"
France	8.33	"
Germany, Holland and Belgium	7.02	"
Spanish America	4.49	"
Denmark, Sweden, Italy and Norway	1.84	"
Austrio, Russia and Portugal	0.15	"
China, Rio Congo and San Domingo	0.04	"
	99.81	
Mercantile Depot	0.19	
	100.00	

The United States has more than a third of the whole, amounting to over fifty millions of dollars a year. Yet the taxes on American products and trade are very heavy. Flour, for example, pays a duty of ten dollars a barrel, while on flour from Spain only two dollars are imposed. Cuba looks chiefly to America for breadstuffs, and takes largely from this country dry goods, agricultural implements, machinery of every description, articles of cooperage and many other things. Then, independent of all this, a large American tonnage is employed which enlarges the commerce and brings great profits to the shipping and merchants of the United States. It is estimated that five thousand vessels of all classes enter the ports of Cuba in a year. Yet, this valuable trade will be lost if the United States does not interfere to stop the work of devastation now going on, by securing the independence of the island. But an imperfect idea can be formed of the vastly increased value of that trade to this country should Cuba become free or annexed. The crowds of enterprising Americans that would go there and develope the resources of the island, to say nothing of the number of invalids and pleasure seekers that would visit this tropical paradise in the winter season, the vast sums of money that Cubans would spend in the United States, and the increased exports and imports under free trade and free intercourse, would make it a most valuable possession. It might well be called the gem of the Antilles for American interests. Indeed it would be of far greater value to the commerce of the world generally than it is now.

The products of Cuba, according to the statistics of Don Francisco Fernandez Corredor, which have something of an official character, are as follows :

63,380 houses, annual rent	$16,260,060
3,285 cattle haciendas, 270,798 bullocks and cows, 35,200 horses and mares, 3,342 mules and asses, 349,960 hogs, 34,813 sheep and goats,	5,286,180
1,365 sugar estates, producing 1,127,351,750 lbs. with molasses, rum, and savings attached to the culture	67,641,105
996 coffee estate, producing 16,822.000 lbs	2,523.300
9,482 vegas of tobacco, prod'g 69,030.000 lbs.	16,912,500
Wax, 5,227,600 lbs...............................	1,794,384
Honey, 362,276 barrels	1.226.966
5,738 pasture grounds, and 21,842 farms, producing	
4,902,525 lbs. cocoa...............................	
500,000 " cotton	
125,000 " arrowroot	
50,000,000 " rice	
7,329,425 " beans	
7,500,000 " potatoes	
1,025 " indigo	13,748.746
2,000,000 " scroons of plantains.................	
2,192,775 " cheese	
125,000,000 " nourishing roots or vegetables.........	
70,000 loads of greens.......................	
1,000,000 " maloja, or corn grn. fodder...........	
240,000,000 lbs. of corn............................	
Ginger, Palm Leaf, rope bark (majagua) bituminous coal, (chapapote).................................	1,000,000
Fruits, milk, starch, poultry and eggs 3,836,866	
Brick manufacturers, block quarries 1,419,000	
Timber..1,380,000	
Fisheries..1,000,000	
Copper ore.................................... 984,587	
	8,620.453
106,088 separate estates, urban or rustic and 20,156 establishments of industry and commerce; anonymous companies, professions, arts, and trades..	124,469,117
Total amount of products and annual incomes,	$259,522,811

It was estimated by the Commissioners at Madrid in 1867 much higher. After making a liberal deduction it amounted according to their statistics, to :—$307,500,000.

No estimate has been made, as far as known, of the total value of the developed property on the island, but taking the products as a basis, and the estimate of products given above is less, doubtless, than the actual amount, the value must be near two thousand millions of dollars. What, for instance, must be the value of the sugar plantations which yield sixty-seven millions of dollars a year, or of the tobacco plantations which give seventeen millions ? But these are only the developed resources of Cuba. The undeveloped resources—those that might, and would, no doubt, be brought out, if the island belonged to the United States, are almost incalculable. The whole area of Cuba embraces over twenty-five millions of acres of land, or according to General Dulce, there is in the island proper over twenty-one millions of acres. Less than fifteen per cent. is under cultivation, and less than twenty-eight per cent. pasture lands. The wood lands cover more than thirty-seven per cent. Probably three or four times the amount now under cultivation could be cultivated. No doubt the sugar and tobacco productions could be increased two or three hundred per cent. or more, and would give this country, in the case of annexation, the complete monopoly of these products in the world. Besides the productions peculiar to the tropics, including a great variety and abundance of fruits, Cuba produces in the high lands the apple, pear, peach, fig, grape, as well as wheat, rye, barley and other things of the temperate zone. It is hardly necessary to mention the wonderful variety of medicinal and aromatic plants, the fine mahogany, cedar, and other valuable woods, or the abundant resources in minerals and stones—as of copper, lead, iron, coal, marble, asphaltum, jasper, agate, opal and other things, for their existence is generally known. Enough has been said to show that there is no spot on the globe richer or more valuable than Cuba in resources to a country like the United States which knows so well how to use them.

Spain derives a revenue of about thirty-seven millions of dollars a year from Cuba. Six to ten millions of this, according to circumstances, go to the government of the old country, and the rest is taken by Spanish officials, and for the support of an insufferable

Spanish despotism on the island. The Cubans—the people from whom this vast amount is wrung—get none of it, and have no control over a dollar of it. The tax on the city and rural revenue of the Cuban people is over fourteen per cent., and this is in addition to the high import and export duties. It is calculated that the Spanish rulers over Cuba intend to draw for the year ending July, 1870, fifty to sixty millions of dollars from the suffering Cubans.

It may be proper to mention under this head that no island or country in the world has more excellent harbors than Cuba. There are more than twenty, besides a number of bays, into which shipping can go. Nine of these, namely, Havana, Bahia, Honda, Nuevitas, Nipe, Levisa, Guantanamo, St. Jago de Cuba, and Cienfuegos will admit ships of the largest class, and some of them are the finest and best protected harbors on the globe. The value of these to commerce is very great, but in addition to that, they are of the highest importance in a naval point of view.

The Population and Character of it.

The population of Cuba, according to the last census of June, 1862, showed there were:

WHITES—EUROPEAN STOCK—Males	403,337	
" " " Females	326,620	—729,957
" YUCATESE—Males	507	
" " Females	236—	743
" CHINESE—Males	34,025	
" " Females	25—	34,050
TOTAL WHITES		764,750
COLORED—FREE—Males	108,097	
" " Females	113,320	—221,417
" CAPTURED EMANCIPADOS—Males	3,171	
" " Females	1,350—	4,521
" SLAVES—Males	220,305	
" " Females	148,245	—368,550
TOTAL COLORED		594,488

RECAPITULATION.

WHITES	764,750
COLORED	594,488
GRAND TOTAL	1,359,238

Fernandez Corredor made the population something more; and considering the increase since the census of 1862 there is now, probably, a million and a half inhabitants on the island.

One feature of the population is worthy of particular notice, and that is, that over six hundred thousand of the people are native whites of pure European stock. There has not been, as in Mexico, Central America, and some of the South American States, a mixture with Indians, for there were no Indians left in Cuba, and there has been little amalgamation with the negroes. The existence of slavery and the pride of race naturally prevented the mixture of whites and negroes to any considerable extent. Of all the so-called Spanish American countries or colonies, not one can boast of a higher or more intellectual type of people than Cuba.

In an article in the *North American Review*, January, 1849, on the poetry of Spanish America, attributed to Longfellow, the following language is used with reference to the people of Cuba : " Passing eastward across the Gulf, our eyes rest on the Queen of the Antilles, on fair and glorious Cuba, that 'summer isle of Eden,' whose name fills the mind with the most enchanting pictures of tropical beauty, the most delicious dreams of splendor and luxury and magnificent ease—that garden of the West, gorgeous with perpetual flowers, and brilliant with the plumage of innumerable birds, beneath whose glowing sky the teeming earth yields easy and abundant harvest to the toil of man, and whose capacious harbors invite the commerce of the world. In this island, so richly endowed with material gifts, we find the noblest and loftiest poets of Spanish America, men of true and universal sympathies, of high aspiration and heroic character, whose souls are fired with great ideas and unselfish hopes, whose poems are not stereotyped sentimentalities, tender or terrible, but manly outpourings of serious feeling, full of a genuine, high-toned enthusiasm for great and generous objects."

Out of the seven to eight hundred thousand whites of European stock, there are not more than a hundred thousand Spaniards, including thirty or forty thousand troops, and numbers of officials. All the rest are native Cubans. The total colored, or negro, population, apart from the comparatively few Chinese and Yucatese, as shown by the table given above, was a little less than six hundred thousand. Out of this, according to the census of 1862, two hundred and twenty-one thousand were free. The slaves at that time numbered three hundred and sixty-eight thousand.

But slavery no longer exists in Cuba, except where the Spanish government is in power and maintains it. The Cuban revolutionary government has abolished it. This is particularly worthy of notice, because the fact may not be generally known in the United States, and because it has been denied by a distinguished member of the American Congress. When the revolution commenced the leaders contemplated the gradual abolition of slavery. In the declaration of independence, on the 10th of October, 1868, the Cubans declare : " We desire the gradual abolition of slavery with indemnification." But they soon advanced beyond this, and, therefore, in the constitution of the Cuban Republic, adopted on the 10th of April, 1869, it is declared, in article 24, "*All the inhabitants of the republic of Cuba are absolutely free.*" This question, then, is set at rest forever, so far as the Cuban revolution or the Cubans can settle it. Slavery can only continue to exist on the island through Spanish power. This fact alone ought to make the statesmen of the United States, and particularly those of the republican party, warm friends of the Cuban cause.

Nature of the Spanish Government in Cuba.

Throughout the whole history of Cuba the Spanish government has been a pure, unmitigated military despotism. The few brief and spasmodic concessions of reform or change hardly amount to an exception, for the government has invariably fallen back to the old despotism, and instead of any improvement for the better, the oppression of the Cubans has gone on from bad to worse. Every branch of the administration has been always under the absolute control of the Captain-General—a power with which he has been invested by the home government. Ever since the close of the war of independence of the South American States, he has been clothed by special law with all the powers given to commanders of besieged places. The following royal decree, issued at Madrid, May 28, 1825, has been the basis of the government over Cuba:

" His Majesty, the King our Lord, desiring to obviate the inconveniences which might result, in extraordinary cases, from a division of command and from the interferences of powers and prerogatives of the respective officers; for the important end of preserving in that precious island (Cuba) his legitimate sovereign authority and the public tranquility, through proper means, has resolved, in accordance with the opinion of his council of ministers, *to give to your excellency the fullest authority, bestowing upon you all the powers which by the royal ordinances are granted to the governors of besieged cities.* In consequence of this, his majesty gives to your excellency *the most ample and unbounded power, not only to send away from the island any persons in office, whatever be their occupation, rank, class, or condition,* whose continuance therein your excellency may deem injurious, or whose *conduct, public or private, may alarm you,* replacing them with persons faithful to his majesty, and deserving of all the confidence of your excellency; but also to suspend the execution of any order whatsoever, or any general provision *made concerning any branch of the administration,* as your excellency may think most suitable to the royal service."

In accordance with this decree, Cuba was under martial law until 1860. A modification of the administrative system was then made, but this lasted only for a short time. In 1867 Captain-General Lersundi virtually re-established martial law in the island, and had even the plainest civil cases tried by military commissions. These commissions generally were composed of stupid and ignorant officers of the army, who, trampling upon all law, often sentenced to death or hard labor innocent men, and acquitted the worst criminals for money. Heavy taxes have been imposed without the Cubans having a voice in the matter, and if any one ventured to remonstrate with the home government he was looked upon as a rebel. The Cubans have been excluded from all offices, except such as were insignificant or unprofitable; while their property, liberty, and even their lives were at the mercy of their relentless rulers.

This tyrannical and barbarous system, which brought about the present revolution, was abolished by Captain-General Dulce, but only for a short period. He fell back to it with greater severity, for since then even sham trials have been dispensed with, and only his will while he was in Cuba, or the will of the Spanish volunteers was the law to imprison, banish, or execute any suspected Cuban.

The judges and other civil officers of the government have always been either corrupt or the most ignorant men of Spain—men who only came to Cuba to make money. In numerous instances their offices have been left in the hands of underlings and clerks to transact business.

The collection of the revenue has been in the hands of ignorant and corrupt men, who, from the highest to the lowest officer, have always plundered the treasury. Nearly, if not fully, two-thirds of the revenue has been generally embezzled or stolen.

Of late the government, the revenue, the high courts of justice, and the Captain-General himself, have fallen into the hands of a mob, known as the Volunteers, who rule over whatever is left to Spain in Cuba.

At present the so called Spanish Government in Cuba is anarchical and as revolutionary as that of the patriots, only not in so good a cause. The volunteers, that is, the Spaniards, numbering less than a twentieth of the whole population, deposed the late

Captain-General Dulce, and by this revolution usurped the authority over the island. This revolutionary faction is virtually the ruling power in Cuba now. A significant trait of the present rule of the volunteers at Havana is the announcement of a determination to hold the power now in their hands, whatever government be established in Spain, and to reject particularly the republican form, and any decree favorable to the emancipation of the slaves. In fact, the present accidental ruling Spanish power in Cuba has no legitimate origin, and does not protect life and property. Poland has been called the Niobe of nations, and how truthfully might Cuba be called the Niobe of colonies. There is not in the civilized world a more despotic government than that over Cuba. It belongs rather to the dark ages than this age. It is a disgrace to our enlightened times, and a foul blot upon free republican America. Such a vile government which treats free white men as slaves, and which would perpetuate African slavery if it could, should not be suffered to exist in any part of the civilized world and should certainly be driven from American soil.

Efforts of the Cubans for Freedom.

The earliest effort of the Cubans for freedom was about the time the Spanish colonies of South America acquired their independence. Venezeula, which was then at war with Spain, was fitting out an expedition to help the Cubans, but the United States opposed the movement. Mr. Clay explained in a speech the motive for this opposition. It was feared that the independence of Cuba at that time would lead to the abolition of negro slavery in the island, and that this would affect the institution in the Southern States of this country. Thus, it will be seen, the United States was mainly instrumental in preventing Cuban independence long ago, and that it owes something to the poor Cubans for this selfish and cruel conduct. Cuba has been suffering under a relentless tyranny ever since, though still endeavoring at times to shake it off. Her endeavors have brought about not only the persecution and even execution of many illustrious Cubans, but also that of high-minded Spaniards, such as General Lorenzo, who, while Governor of Santiago de Cuba in 1836, proclaimed there the liberal constitution promulgated in Spain, for which Captain-General Tacon sent from Havana a heavy body of troops against him and his constitutional followers. Several years later many Cubans, who remonstrated against the slave trade, were persecuted for having done so, and nearly all of them driven into exile. Shortly, thereafter, military commissions were set at work all over the Western Department of Cuba to suppress an alleged conspiracy among the colored people. The guilty parties were found chiefly among the rich free colored men, whose property was, of course, confiscated, and their lives taken by wholesale on the scaffold, while not a few of them died under the lash, which was freely and mercilessly used to compel them to confession. The suppression of this alleged conspiracy was followed a few years later by a real conspiracy of the white people under the lead of Gen. Lopez, who, being detected before his plans were matured for an uprising in the central part of the island, fled and came to the United States. In 1850 he renewed his efforts and sailed from the United States, at the head of some six hundred men, and landed at Cardenas. He failed in this attempt to free Cuba, and returned to the United States. During the subsequent year partial uprisings took place, and Lopez sailed for Cuba once more, with about 450 men, to assist his friends to achieve their independence; but he again failed, and he, with many of his followers, were executed. However, the Cubans, persevering in their determination to be free, renewed their plans to that end, and a well organized movement was started under Gen. Quitman, but fell through in 1855, with the loss of valuable lives, and the banishment of many distinguished Cubans, to say nothing of a heavy outlay of money. Nevertheless, the Cubans did not despair, and a few years afterward, began to work again for their freedom, but suddenly stopped to listen to liberal propositions from Spain, whither a delegation was sent in 1866. After a protracted stay, and long deliberations at Madrid, the delegation returned home disgusted, and reported to their constituents that nothing was to be expected from Spain in the way of liberal reforms or justice to Cuba. Then the Cubans recommenced their interrupted work, and when the late Spanish revolution broke out they were maturing their plans to free Cuba from the military sway of Spain. That revolution improved their opportunity, and on the 10th of October, 1868, they rose up in arms, and made a declaration of independence, dated at Manzanillo on that day. The following are extracts from that instrument:

" In arming ourselves against the tyrannical government of Spain, we must, according to precedent in all civilized countries, proclaim before the world, the cause that impels us to take this step, which, though likely to entail considerable disturbances upon the present, will insure the happiness of the future.

" It is well known that Spain governs the island of Cuba with an iron and blood-stained hand. The former holds the latter deprived of political, civil and religious liberty. Hence the unfortunate Cubans being illegally prosecuted and thrown into exile, or executed by military commissions in times of peace: hence their being kept from public meeting, and forbidden to speak or write on affairs of State: hence their remonstrances against the evils that afflict them, being looked upon as the proceedings of rebels, from the fact that they are bound to keep silence and obey: hence the never-ending plague of hungry officials from Spain, to devour the product of their industry and labor: hence their exclusion from public stations and want of opportunity to skill themselves in the art of government: hence the restrictions to which public instruction with them is subjected, in order to keep them so ignorant as not to be able to know and enforce their rights in any shape or form whatever:

hence the navy and standing army which are kept upon their country at an enormous expenditure from their own wealth, to make them bend their knees and submit their necks to the iron yoke that disgraces them: hence the grinding taxation under which they labor, and which would make them all perish in misery but for the marvellous fertility of their soil. On the other hand, Cuba cannot prosper as she ought to, because white immigration, that suits her best, is artfully kept from her shores by the Spanish Government. And as Spain has many a time promised us, Cubans, to respect our rights, without having hitherto fulfilled her promises; as she continues to tax us heavily, and by so doing is likely to destroy our wealth; as we are in danger of losing our property, our lives and our honor under further Spanish domination; as we have reached a depth of degradation unutterably revolting to manhood; as great nations have sprung from revolt against a similar disgrace after exhausted pleading for relief; as we despair of justice from Spain through reasoning, and cannot longer live deprived of the rights which other people enjoy, we are constrained to appeal to arms to assert our rights in the battle-field, cherishing the hope that our grievances will be a sufficient excuse for this last resort to redress them and secure our future welfare.

"To the God of our conscience and to all civilized nations we submit the sincerity of our purpose. Vengeance does not mislead us, nor is ambition our guide. We only want to be free, and see all men with us equally free, as the Creator intended mankind to be. Our earnest belief is that all men are brethren. Hence our love of toleration, order and justice in every respect. We desire the gradual abolition of slavery with indemnification; we admire universal suffrage, as it insures the sovereignty of the people; we demand a religious regard for the inalienable rights of man, as the basis of freedom and national greatness."

Review of the Insurrectionary Movement.

The Cuban patriots first rose at Demajagua, in the district of Yara, and, as was said before, on the 10th of October, 1868. On that eventful day there were only one hundred and twenty men to start the movement in this locality, and they had but few fire-arms. Three days after, the districts of Bayamo, Manzanillo, Jiguani and Las Tunas rose also, and the ranks of the liberators swelled to four thousand men. Some were armed with fowling-pieces, others with old flint-lock guns, not a few with pruning knives fastened to long sticks, some with pistols, and the majority with cutlasses, and whatever they could get. Such was the beginning of this heroic struggle.

Shortly afterwards the insurrection spread over the districts of Holguin, Palma Soriano, Cobre, and Santiago de Cuba in the Eastern Department, and at the same time it was spreading over the whole of the Central Department. The want of arms and other materials of war caused the insurrection to drag along, but it continued to extend farther and wider, and soon embraced Palmilla and Saguey Grande in the Western Department. At the end of one year the patriots had risen in and had overrun nearly two-thirds of the whole island. More than forty thousand are now in the field, and though poorly armed for the most part, are successfully contending against the Spanish troops, which are well armed with the best approved weapons of the United States.

But a small amount of war materials has reached the patriots on account of the difficulties met with by their agents abroad. The restriction placed upon their actions in the United States, under the construction given to the neutrality laws, has amounted, in some instances, almost to persecution. Perhaps not more than two hundred Americans have been able to join the patriots in Cuba, in consequence of the strict vigilance of their government, though thousands have been eager and ready to go.

The means used up to the present time to forward the revolution are from the Cubans alone; nobody else has helped the cause with funds.

The districts of Santiago de Cuba, Guantanama, Holguin, Manzanillo, Jiguani, Bayamo, Las Tunas, Puerto Principe, Nuevitas, Santa Clara, Santa Cruz, Moron, Remedios, Trinidad, Santo Espiritu, Sagua, Cienfuegos and Colon, are controlled by the patriots, with the exception of a few towns and villages within these districts, where the Spanish troops are kept at bay and deprived of any other means of attack than by increased reinforcements from Spain. Want of war materials alone prevents the patriots from capturing their besieged enemies, even in those intrenched places where they are supplied through the seaboard and under the protection of the navy. Hence the determination of the Cubans to burn the sugar plantations, so as to deprive their enemies of the means relied upon to carry on the war, and to make the island valueless to them. This, to some extent, will be a set-off for the want of war materials. Were the Cubans as well armed as the Spaniards, the contest would soon be ended and the independence of the island established. The devastation now threatened, and necessary as a war measure with the Cubans, might then be avoided. The determination to burn the plantations, and the whole conduct of the patriots, show how terribly in earnest they are to conquer their independence. A people who would rather see their beloved country in ruins than submit any longer to despotism and political slavery, are not likely to fail in their object. And as Spain is in revolution herself, and too poor to carry on the war without resources from Cuba, there can be little doubt of the success of the Cubans ultimately, though utter desolation may come with it.

The reported expressions of attachment to Spain by wealthy Cubans, as published in the Havana newspapers, are only sham manifestations of loyalty, extorted at the point of the bayonet by the Spanish officials and volunteers, for political effect abroad, and for the purpose of deceiving the people and government of Spain. The revolution is in every Cuban heart throughout the whole island, and as soon as the Cubans have arms enough to confront their enemies at every point, this will be shown. It would be strange, indeed, if any Cubans could be found devoted to a government which denies them the smallest measure of liberty, and which has always cruelly oppressed them. No, there are no Cubans who do not sigh for freedom, whose hearts do not swell at the thought of independence, except, perhaps, a very few renegade paid agents of the Spanish Government.

It is estimated that there are in the revolted districts sixty thousand men, besides the thirty to forty thousand now in the field, ready to join the patriot army as soon as arms can be put in their hands. The whole force even in these districts could thus be raised to ninety or a hundred thousand men—a force, if properly armed, large enough to drive the Spaniards from every part of the island, except in a few places where they might be protected by ships of war. There have been a number of conflicts of arms all along between the Cubans and Spaniards, and although there have not been any battles on a very large scale, several considerable engagements have taken place. The Cubans have shown great bravery as well as skill in these conflicts, which have resulted in general favorably to them. Of course, the Cubans pursue what is called the Fabian policy in war, as General Washington did in the war of American independence, and as all revolutionists do who at first have comparatively limited means for warfare. This is effective war, nevertheless, and succeeds better in the case of a revolted colony like that of Cuba, or of the revolted American colonies, than any other mode of warfare. It proves exhaustive to the enemy which draws its resources and men from a distance, and strengthens the native revolutionists. It is unreasonable, therefore, to ask of the insurgents to make decisive pitched battles on a large scale as a condition for recognizing them as belligerents. The fact alone that Spain is compelled to strain all her means, and to send out continually reinforcements of troops from the old country to keep up the war, and that, too, after the conflict has been raging over a year, shows the magnitude of the struggle and the ability of the Cubans to sustain it. Looking at the progress of the revolution since it commenced, at the augmenting forces of the patriots, and the increasing area of territory over which they are spreading, and at the declining power of Spain over the island, the Cubans have every reason to expect success, and to claim the right of being recognized as a belligerent power. There can be found few examples in history in which a people fighting for their independence have accomplished as much within so short a time as the Cubans.

The Cuban Constitution and Government.

The Constitution adopted by the Constitutional Convention assembled for the purpose of making one, and unanimously approved by the Cuban Congress at Guimaro, the Provisional capital of the Republic, on the tenth day of April, 1869, is as follows:

ARTICLE I. The Legislative Power shall be vested in a House of Representatives.

II. To this Body shall be delegated an equal representation from each of the four States into which the island of Cuba shall be divided.

III. These States are *Oriente*, *Camaguey*, *Las Villas*, and *Occidente*.

IV. No one shall be eligible as Representative of any of these States except a citizen of the Republic who is upward of 20 years of age.

V. No representative of any State shall hold any other official position during his representative term.

VI. Whenever a vacancy occurs in the representation of any State, the Executive thereof shall have power to fill such vacancy until the ensuing election.

VII. The House of Representatives shall elect a President of the Republic, a General-in-Chief of its armies, a President of the Congress, and other executive officers. The General-in-Chief shall be subordinate to the Executive, and shall render him an account of the performance of his duties.

VIII. The President of the Republic, the General-in-Chief, and the members of the House of Representatives, are amenable to charges which may be made by any citizen to the House of Representatives, who shall proceed to examine into the charges preferred; and if, in their judgment, it be necessary, the case of the accused shall be submitted to the Judiciary.

IX. The House of Representatives shall have full power to dismiss from office any functionary whom they have appointed.

X. The legislative acts and decisions of the House of Representatives, in order to be valid and binding, must have the sanction of the President of the Republic.

XI. If the President fail to approve the acts and decisions of the House, he shall, without delay, return the same, with his objections thereto, for the reconsideration of that body.

XII. Within ten days after their reception, the President shall return all bills, resolutions and enactments which may be sent to him by the House for his approval, with his sanction thereof, or with his objections thereto.

XIII. Upon the passage of any act, bill, or resolution, after a reconsideration thereof by the House, it shall be sanctioned by the President.

XIV. The House of Representatives shall legislate upon taxation, public loans, and ratifications of treaties; and shall have power to declare and conclude war, to authorize the President to issue Letters of Marque, to raise troops and provide for their support, to organize and maintain a navy, and to regulate reprisals as to the public enemy.

XV. The House of Representatives shall remain in permanent session from the time of the ratification of this fundamental law by the people, until the termination of the war with Spain.

XVI. The Executive power shall be vested in the President of the Republic.

XVII. No one shall be eligible to the Presidency who is not a native of the Republic, and over 30 years of age.

XVIII. All treaties made by the President may be ratified by the House of Representatives.

XIX. The President shall have power to appoint ambassadors, ministers-plenipotentiary, and consuls of the Republic to foreign countries.

XX. The President shall treat with embassadors, and shall see that the laws are faithfully executed. He shall also issue official commissions to all the functionaries of the Republic.

XXI. The President shall propose the names for the members of his Cabinet to the House of Representatives for its approval.

XXII. The Judiciary shall form an independent co-ordinate department of the Government, under the organization of a special law.

XXIII. Voters are required to possess the same qualifications as to age and citizenship as the Members of the House of Representatives.

XXIV. All the inhabitants of the Republic of Cuba are absolutely *free*.

XXV. All the citizens are considered as soldiers of the Liberating army.

XXVI. The Republic shall not bestow dignities, titles, nor special privileges.

XXVII. The citizens of the Republic shall not accept honors nor titles from foreign countries.

XXVIII. The House of Representatives shall not abridge the freedom of religion, nor of the press, nor of public meetings, nor of education, nor of petition, nor any inalienable right of the people.

XXIX. This Constitution can be amended only by the unanimous concurrence of the House of Representatives.

.Here follow the signatures of Carlos Manuel de Cespedes, President of the Convention, and of all of the Delegates.

We, the undersigned, hereby certify and declare that the foregoing is a correct and faithful translation of the Cuban Constitution, and of each and every Article and clause thereof, and that the same is the fundamental and supreme law of the Republic.

Done by order of the Junta Cubana, at the City of New York, in the United States of America, this 17th day of November, A. D. 1869, and the second year of the Independence of Cuba.

MIGUEL DE ALDAMA,
President.

J. M. MESTRE, *Secretary.*

The government of the republic of Cuba is democratic and federal, as is seen by the Constitution. It shows too that slavery is forever abolished.

The Cabinet is composed of the President of the Republic, a . Secretary of State, a Secretary of War, a Secretary of the Interior and Treasury.

In all the territory controlled by the patriots there are Courts of justice, Post Offices, and a perfect interior organization to execute the laws of the Republic.

The Cuban government has in the United States a special Envoy with full powers to represent it, at Washington, to make loans, and to do other things in behalf of the Republic.

The Cuban Junta has been appointed by this Envoy to assist him in the service of the Republic. The appointment of said Junta has been approved by the Cuban government.

In every department the government is properly constructed, efficient in administration, and commands the respect and obedience of the people. The President, Cespedes, has proved himself to be a man of great ability and equal to the crisis that has brought him to the head of the government. He is assisted, too, both by able civil officers and competent military commanders. It is, then, in all respects, a *de facto* government, which deserves the respect and recognition of the nations of the world, particularly of the United States and the other republics of America which are interested in the development and perpetuation of republican institutions in this hemisphere.

Position of the United States toward Cuba in the Past and at Present.

It has been shown in the foregoing pages that Cuba might have become independent and a republic, shortly after the Spanish South American colonies acquired their freedom, and would have been aided in the effort by these new American republics, had not the United States checked the movement. The motive for this policy on the part of the United States sprung from the fear that in the event of Cuba becoming independent, negro slavery would be abolished in the island, and, that, on account of the proximity of Cuba, this might prove dangerous to the "peculiar institution" in the Southern States.

Little was done by this country with regard to Cuba from that period, 1820-22, until the presidency of Mr. Polk, except to prevent the island falling into the possession of England, France, or any other European Power. During Mr. Polk's administration, the American Minister at Madrid was instructed to ascertain if Spain was disposed to transfer Cuba to the United States for a liberal pecuniary consideration. Spain was not disposed, and no great effort was made to induce her to part with the island. Then, in 1854, the famous Ostend conference was held with a view to press Spain to sell Cuba to the United States. The three American Ministers abroad, who composed this conference, Mr. Buchanan, Mr. Mason and Mr. Soule, strongly recommended the acquisition of Cuba. Mr. Soule, the Minister at Madrid, was instructed to open negotiations with the Spanish Government to that end. It was said the United States Government was disposed to pay the large sum of a hundred and fifty millions to two hundred millions of dollars for Cuba. But Spain would not listen to the proposition, and the project failed. At this point the subject was dropped, though Mr. Buchanan, when President, was disposed to renew the offer to purchase if an opportunity had occurred. From the time of Mr. Polk and all along to near the end of Mr. Buchanan's term, the Southern States and people of the South wished to acquire Cuba for the purpose of strengthening the institution of slavery and increasing the political power of the slaveholding section of the Union. This, in fact, was one of the strongest motives which led to the efforts to purchase Cuba. It was during these years, too, that several expeditions of Cubans and American sympathizers were organized in this country to revolutionize the island and to make it independent of Spain. Those of General Lopez and General Quitman were the principal ones. They failed, as will be remembered, chiefly on account of the vigilance of the United States Government in enforcing the neutrality laws.

Scarcely anything had been said or thought of Cuba since Mr. Buchanan's presidency, for the people of this country were absorbed in their own civil war and its consequences, till the revolution in Spain and the rising of the Cubans brought the subject prominently before the American public and government again. This time it is not a filibustering expedition or the effort of a few Cuban refugees and American sympathizers to free the island from Spanish rule. It is a grand and wide spread movement of the Cubans themselves on their own soil. Indeed, it has assumed such proportions and the revolutionary feeling is so strong every where that this movement may be called an universal one. The success of the revolution in Spain, which drove Queen Isabella from the throne, and changed the government of the mother country, inspired the Cubans to follow the revolutionary example set them. They resolved to shake off the intolerable despotism of their Spanish masters, knowing that whatever might be the change of government at Madrid, there would be no hope for them—that they would be kept in political slavery and under military rule.

The first appeal of the Cubans for sympathy and recognition was to the United States. They sent an envoy to the government at Washington to represent their case, and they commissioned several of their eminent fellow patriots, known here as the Cuban Junta, to aid the revolution. But the former has not been received officially, and only as a private individual, though with much kindness and many expressions of sympathy, while obstructions and difficulties have been thrown in the way of the latter in their efforts to serve the cause of their country. Yet, how different are the circumstances connected with the present revolutionary movement to those associated with all previous movements for the independence of Cuba. No party in the United States now desires the annexation of Cuba to strenghten the institution of slavery, for slavery has been abolished both here and in Cuba— that is, in Cuba as far as the action and power of the revolutionary government go. Spain alone sustains slavery, and wherever her power ceases to operate there are no more slaves. The present movement, therefore, is in the interest of universal freedom for all races, as well as for emancipation from Spanish despotism. Then, how insignificant were all previous movements for Cuban independence, by expeditions from the United States or otherwise, compared to this one. It has, indeed, attained the character of a grand national movement.

From whatever point of view the Cuban revolution is looked at the position the American Government has occupied with regard to it appears anomalous, weak, unkind, and in conflict with sound policy. The Cuban republic has been recognized by one independent American nation, and several others have acknowledged the Cubans as a belligerent power; yet the United States Government, which ought to have been first in taking such a step, continues to give a cold shoulder to the Cubans.

It is time the administration at Washington should see the value of Cuba to this country, if it can become independent or annexed before it is utterly desolated by war, and see, too, that no better opportunity can arise for securing its independence or acquisition. Hence the instructions given last spring to General Sickles, the American Minister at Madrid, to make another proposition for the purchase of the island. A hundred millions of dollars were offered, but this time in the form of a purchase by the Cubans themselves, under a guarantee of the United States for the payment. This, doubtless, was considered a delicate way of making the offer in order to save the *amour propre* of the Spaniards and Spanish government in the case of a sale being made. Again the government of Spain refused to listen to such a proposition, and begged the American Minister to withdraw the communication embodying it as an official document. It was evident, the revolutionary government of Spain, whatever might have been the views or wish of the individual members of it, was afraid to entertain the offer. It was not very securely seated in power, had a formidable opposition arrayed against it, which might have made the Cuban question the fulcrum of hostility, and was looking to political ambition in the future. The members of that government were not prepared to risk so much by the sale of Cuba, though common sense and the condition of things both in the island and at home might have taught them that this would have been the best solution of the difficulty. Thus, it is seen, this last effort to secure the independence of Cuba in a friendly way has failed, as all former efforts failed.

Since the Spanish Government rejected this proposal, it has exhibited a remarkable friendly tone to the United States, and overwhelming politeness to the American Minister at Madrid. And this seems to have had a very soothing effect upon the administration at Washington, particularly upon certain members of it. But is it not known that all this overstrained politeness is mere pretence, and that Spain, like nearly all the old countries of Europe, has no love for the American republic and would do anything to check its progress and growing power? Are there not evidences, and that of a recent date, too, that she has been ready to interpose in American affairs for the purpose of destroying republican institutions in this hemisphere? Why, then is so much consideration shown to Spanish sensibilities and interests on this Cuban question? Surely more consideration is due to our neighbors— to the natives of American soil—the heroic Cubans—who appeal with outstretched arms to the American people and government for recognition and aid. The politeness of the State Department to Spain has been withering to American interests and humanity. The punctilious and overstrained regard for the neutrality laws, which are un-American in principle and ought not to exist, is blighting to the proper policy and noble sympathies of this country.

It has been said, and, no doubt, with much truth, that the question of the Alabama claims has had some influence upon the American government and certain public men in Congress, and that this has prevented the recognition of the Cubans and a more vigorous policy in their favor. How selfish and weak this appears! How humiliating to this mighty republic, which should and ought to make laws for itself on all American questions! But there is no parallel between the hasty recognition of an integral portion of the United States as belligerents by England, and the recognition by this country of the Cubans—a distant colony of Spain and an American people—after fourteen or fifteen months of successful warfare. Nor should the American Government be deterred from performing a duty, which humanity and sound national policy call for, by any such consideration. But if this great question, which appeals to the pride and hearts of the American people, and which involves the interest and progress of the republic, is to be reduced simply to one of present profit or loss, the balance will be greatly in favor of Cuba. That island is worth far more than the Alabama claims. But really there is no such question—it is a mere bugbear. The United States can take Cuba and settle the Alabama claims afterwards at its own convenience and in its own way. All the statesmen of the world, except, perhaps, a few public men here who are not worthy of the name, see that Cuba must belong to the United States and that the opportunity for acquiring it has come.

The recent action of the government in seizing the Spanish gunboats, and thereby preventing them from making war on the Cubans, indicates a change of policy. There are indications, too, that the President and Congress will shortly take a decided course in favor of Cuban independence. The country expects this. Public sentiment universally calls for it. And, as this great republic cannot afford to take half measures merely, or to place itself in a position to be humiliated by defeat in whatever it earnestly undertakes, there is hope that the hour of Cuba's freedom is approaching. Such a consummation would do honor to the country, and to the people of all parties who desire it, but especially would it bring glory to the administration and the party in power. The lamented General Rawlins, the President's dear friend, and Secretary of War, comprehended the Cuban question and the position of the government, when, in his dying and touching words, he appealed to Secretary Cresswell for "poor, struggling Cuba," when he declared that "her tyrannical enemies must be crushed, and Cuba must be free." It may well be said, also, as he earnestly expressed the sentiment, this republic is responsible for the fate of Cuba.